**LEGO**

# NINJAGO

### Masters of Spinjitzu

P9-BYL-706

# WAY OF THE NINJA

## ADAPTED BY TRACEY WEST

SCHOLASTIC INC.
NEW YORK   TORONTO   LONDON   AUCKLAND
SYDNEY   MEXICO CITY   NEW DELHI   HONG KONG

ISBN 978-0-545-41877-5

12 11 10 9 8 7 6 5 4 3 2          12 13 14 15 16 17/0

Printed in the U.S.A.          40
This edition first printing, January 2012

# MEET KAI

*Clang! Clang! Clang!*

Kai pounded metal into the shape of a sword. He dipped the hot metal into a bucket of cold water. Then he pulled out . . . a crooked sword.

"You made it too quickly, Kai," said his sister, Nya. "Be patient."

"Don't worry, Nya," Kai said. "I'm going to be a better blacksmith than Dad ever was!"

An old man with a white beard walked into the shop.

"These are tools for a samurai," he said, looking around. "But nothing for a ninja."

"Ninja?" Kai laughed. "There are no ninja in these parts, old man." Kai turned to Nya. When he looked back, the old man was gone.

That night, an army of skeleton warriors roared into Kai's village on their Skull Motorbikes. Their king, Samukai, led them in his Skull Truck.

"Let me go first!" whined Nuckal, a skeleton commander. "I'm dying to go down there!"

"Nitwit! You're already dead!" barked his partner, Kruncha.

"Besides, Master Samukai, you said I could go first," Kruncha added.

"Sorry, boys, this one is mine," Samukai said. "Just find that map!"

Samukai's red eyes gleamed like fire. "Attack!" he yelled.

# ENTER THE SKELETONS

*Vroom! Vroom! Vroom!*
The warriors zoomed into the village on their Skull Motorbikes. Samukai steered the Skull Truck toward Kai's blacksmith shop. The villagers screamed and ran away.

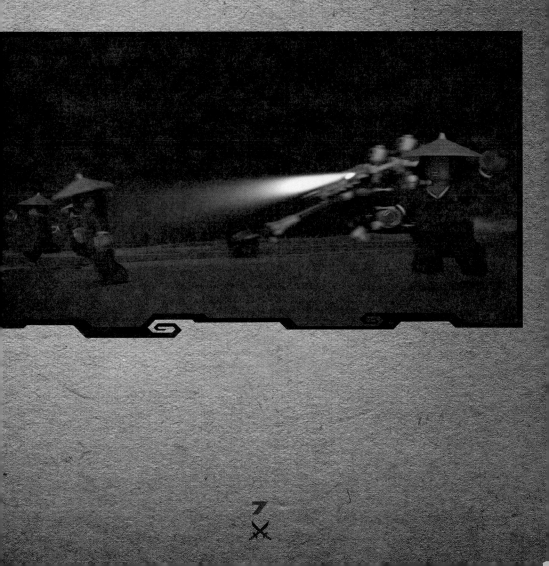

Kai raced out to fight the warriors. He swung his samurai sword, and one of the skeletons' heads popped off.

"Ow!" Kai cried, as the skeleton bit his ankle. "Bite this!"

He kicked the skeleton head like a football. The other warriors clapped as the skull flew through the air.

Nya stepped up and whacked two of the warriors with her staff.

"You should have stayed back," Kai told her.

"And let *you* have all the fun?" Nya asked.

While Kai and Nya fought the skeletons, Nuckal and Kruncha snuck into the blacksmith shop.

Inside Kai's shop, Nuckal put on a samurai hat.
"You're not looking hard enough!" Kruncha
said, bopping him on the head.
"Owww! No, *you're* not looking hard enough!"
cried Nuckal, throwing the helmet at Kruncha.

*Bam! Pow! Crunch!* The two skeletons slapped at each other. Kruncha banged into the wall. The sign over the door fell down.

The two skeletons gasped when they saw something hidden behind the sign. "The map!" they shouted.

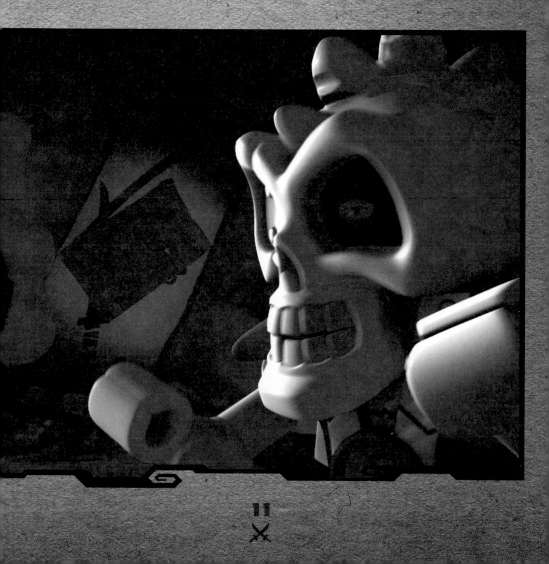

# KAI'S MISSION

Outside, Samukai leaped down from his truck. He grabbed four knives and attacked Kai.

As Kai fell back, a cry rang out. *"Ninjago!"*

A spinning gold tornado whirled between Kai and Samukai. The tornado smacked into Samukai. When it stopped spinning, the old man from the shop stood there.

"Sensei Wu!" cried Samukai. "Your Spinjitzu looks rusty."

With a grin, Samukai threw his knives. They slammed into an old water tower. The tower started to fall.

*"Ninjago!"* With a yell, Sensei Wu spun and picked up Kai before the tower could land on him.

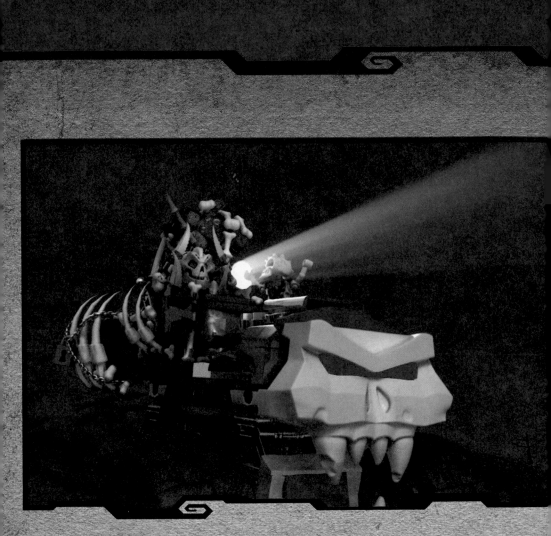

Laughing, Samukai jumped into his truck.
"Garmadon says to get the girl," he growled.
Kruncha pulled a lever. A skeleton claw swung
out of the truck and grabbed Nya! Then the Skull
Truck sped away.

"Nya!" screamed Kai. He picked up his sword. "I'm going to get my sister back."

"Where they go, no mortal may follow," Sensei Wu told him. "That was Samukai, King of the Underworld. If he's working for Lord Garmadon, things are worse than I thought."

# A TALE OF TWO BROTHERS

"Why did they come here? What do they want?" Kai asked.

"Long before time had a name, Ninjago was created by the first Spinjitzu Master," Sensei Wu began. "He used the Four Weapons of Spinjitzu: the Scythe of Quakes, the Nunchuks of Lightning, the Shurikens of Ice, and the Sword of Fire."

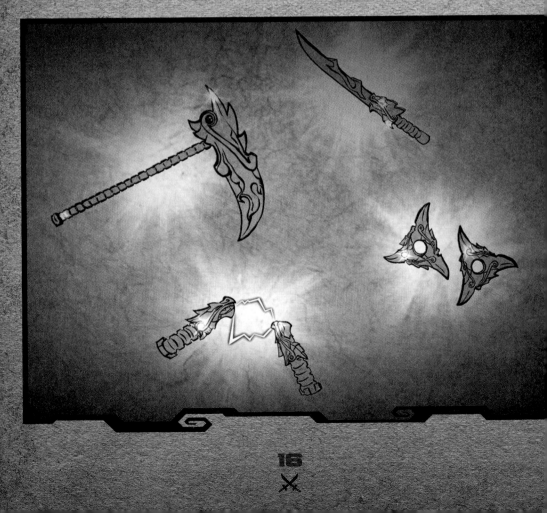

"When the master passed away, his two sons swore to protect them," Sensei Wu went on. "But the oldest was taken over by darkness. He wanted the Weapons for his own. A battle between brothers broke out. The oldest was struck down and sent to the Underworld."

"The younger brother hid the Weapons in four different places," said Sensei Wu. "He sent a Guardian to protect each one. And then he gave the map to an honest man to hide. That honest man was your father."

Kai's eyes grew wide.

"The older brother is Lord Garmadon," Sensei Wu told Kai. "I must find those Weapons before he does!"

"You're the younger brother?" Kai asked. "Then you came here looking for the map?"

Sensei Wu shook his head. "No," he said. "I came for something greater. You!"

"You have the fire inside, Kai," Sensei Wu said. "You can help me."

Kai turned away. "I don't care about all that. I just need to get my sister."

Sensei Wu twirled around and knocked down Kai with his staff. He put his foot on Kai's chest.

"If you want to get your sister back, you must learn to tame the fire inside," said Sensei Wu. "Only if you master Spinjitzu will you be ready to face Lord Garmadon."

Kai knew Sensei Wu was right. Together they began the long journey to Sensei Wu's dojo.

## NINJA-IN-TRAINING

"Complete this training course before I finish my tea," Sensei Wu told Kai. "Then, we will see if you are ready."

Day after day, Kai tried to complete the course. He battled wood soldiers on a spinning platform. But he smacked into one of the soldiers and fell off.

"Fail," Sensei Wu said.

Kai tried to jump across a row of spinning spikes. Once again, he fell.

"Fail," said Sensei Wu.

Kai failed and failed and failed again. But he didn't give up. He kept training.

Finally, Kai got it right. He dodged weapons. He jumped on pillars. He fought wooden soldiers with his sword. And he did it all before the sensei finished his tea.

"So now can I learn Spinjitzu?" Kai asked.

"You already have," Sensei Wu replied. "Your final test comes tomorrow."

# AND THEN THERE WERE FOUR

That night, Kai practiced Spinjitzu while he brushed his teeth.

"Take that! And that! And this!" he cried, spinning around.

Then he stopped. He was surrounded by three ninja dressed in black!

Kai threw his toothbrush at the ninja.
Then he leaped onto a ceiling beam.
One of the ninja jumped in front of him.
 *"Hi-yah!"* Kai cried, knocking him down.
 But another ninja tossed him outside.
Kai landed in the training yard. He made
the platforms and pillars spin.

The spinning platforms slammed into the ninja, but they jumped back to their feet.

*Bam! Pow! Kick!* All three ninja attacked Kai. He fought back bravely.

Sensei Wu's voice rang out. "Stop!"

The three ninja bowed. "Yes, Sensei."

"They're your students, too?" Kai asked, and the sensei nodded. "This was my final test, wasn't it?"

"What is the meaning of this, Master?" one ninja asked.

"Each of you is in tune with a different element," Sensei Wu explained. "But first — *Ninjago!*"

Sensei Wu began to spin. He whirled around the ninja. When he stopped, the ninja were all wearing different uniforms!

Kai wore a red uniform. "Kai, Master of Fire," Sensei Wu said. Then he pointed to a ninja in a blue uniform. "Jay is blue, Master of Lightning."

"Black ninja is Cole," Sensei Wu went on. "Solid as rock. Master of Earth." Finally, he approached the ninja in white. "And white ninja is Zane, Master of Ice."

"You four are the chosen ones who will protect the Weapons of Spinjitzu from Lord Garmadon!" Sensei Wu told them.

"But what about my sister?" demanded Kai.

Jay gasped. "We're saving a girl? Is she cute? Does she like blue?"

"When we find the Weapons, we will find your sister, Kai," Sensei Wu promised. "It is time! We must go to the first Weapon."

Cole stepped up. "Hold on a minute. You said you were going to teach us Spinjitzu."

"Spinjitzu is inside each of you," Sensei Wu replied. "But it will only be unlocked when the key is ready to be found."

"Great! Now we have to find a key," Jay complained.

"I feel like he's taking us for a ride," Cole added.

Kai pulled on his red hood. "If it means finding my sister, then sign me up!"

The four ninja followed Sensei Wu into the night.

# LEGO NINJAGO
## Masters of Spinjitzu

# MASTERS OF SPINJITZU

### ADAPTED BY TRACEY WEST

SCHOLASTIC INC.
NEW YORK   TORONTO   LONDON   AUCKLAND
SYDNEY   MEXICO CITY   NEW DELHI   HONG KONG

ISBN 978-0-545-41877-5

12 11 10 9 8 7 6 5 4 3 2        12 13 14 15 16 17/0

Printed in the U.S.A.                    40
This edition first printing, January 2012

# MEET THE TEAM

As the sun rose over Ninjago, four young ninja pulled a wagon up a tall mountain. They were on a quest to find the Scythe of Quakes, one of the Four Weapons of Spinjitzu.

In the wagon sat Sensei Wu, their teacher.

Kai, the ninja in red, was the newest member of the team.

"So, where did Sensei find you three?" Kai asked the others.

"I was testing my limits," answered Cole, the ninja in black. "I climbed the tallest mountain without any tools. But when I reached the top, Sensei Wu was there, drinking his tea."

"I was testing my invention," said Jay, the ninja in blue.

Jay had made a pair of wings. He tried to fly . . . only to crash and find Sensei Wu there. He was waiting on a nearby rooftop, drinking his tea.

"And I was testing myself," said Zane,
the quiet ninja in white.

Zane was meditating at the bottom of a
frozen lake. And somehow . . . Sensei Wu
was there underwater, drinking his tea!

## THE PLAN

"Stop!" Sensei Wu cried suddenly.

The ninja came to a halt. A large canyon stretched out in front of them. Skeleton warriors were digging into the side of the mountain.

"The Caves of Despair," Sensei said. "Samukai must be close to unearthing the Scythe of Quakes."

"Remember, do not use the Weapon," Sensei Wu warned. "For its power —"

"Yeah, yeah, yeah!" Jay said. He had heard this from Sensei before. "Its power is too much for us mortals." He turned to his friends. "All right guys, let's chop-socky this lemonade stand! Cole, you got the plan?"

"Sure do," Cole replied. "First, we — hey, where's Kai?"

Kai hadn't waited to hear the plan. The ninja saw him sneaking past the skeleton warriors in the canyon.

"Let's go!" Jay cried.

# STEALTH ATTACK

Jay, Cole, and Zane jumped into the canyon. They saw rocks coming out of the caves on a conveyor belt. The skeleton warriors checked each rock, looking for the Scythe of Quakes.

One of the warriors spotted Kai! But before he could cry out, the other ninja jumped him.

*Bam! Pow! Crunch!* Cole, Jay, and Zane made sure the warrior couldn't sound the alarm.

Kai hid behind some big rocks. He looked up at a tall tower in the middle of the canyon. Inside he saw Samukai, King of the Underworld!

"The map!" Kai cried. The map showed where the Four Weapons of Spinjitzu were hidden. Samukai had stolen it from Kai's blacksmith shop.

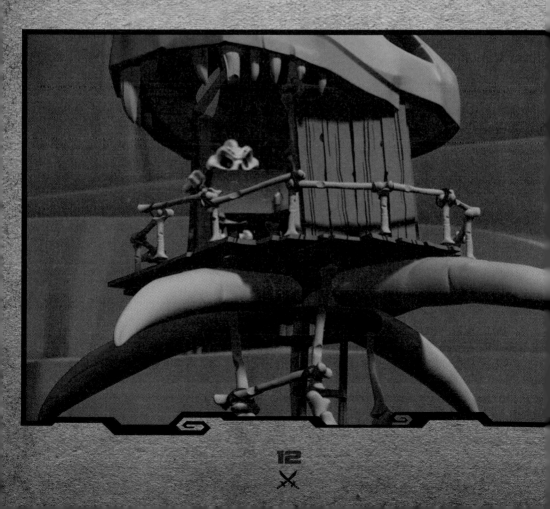

Nearby, two skeleton commanders were checking rocks on the conveyor belt. Cole, Jay, and Zane slid right under them!

But Kruncha and Nuckal didn't notice.

"I found something!" Nuckal cried, holding up a rock.

"That's another rock, you bonehead!" Kruncha yelled.

"But it's shaped like a donut," Nuckal said. "I wonder if it tastes like one?"

*Crunch!* Nuckal bit down hard into the rock. *"Ow!"*

Kai climbed to the top of the tall tower. Cole, Jay, and Zane joined him.

Jay smacked Kai on the head. "What's the matter with you?"

"*Shhh!*" Kai warned. He nodded toward a hole in the tower roof. Inside the tower, Samukai was reading the map.

"It's upside down!" Jay realized. "They're digging in the wrong spot!"

# THE SCYTHE OF QUAKES

"The Golden Weapon is near," Zane realized. He tied a shuriken to a rope and tossed it down the hole. Samukai didn't see it. The shuriken grabbed the map, and Zane pulled it up through the hole.

"There's no time to waste," Kai said. He did a backflip off the tower and ran off.

"What is it with that guy?" Jay asked. "Always in a rush!"

The ninja raced after Kai toward the spot where the Scythe of Quakes was hidden. A big rock blocked the entrance. Cole, Jay, Kai, and Zane worked together to push it aside.

The Scythe of Quakes lit up the dark cave. The Weapon lay on top of a statue of a dragon's head.

"That is so cool!" Jay cried. His voice echoed through the cave.

"*Shh!* Not so loud!" Cole warned. He jumped on top of the statue, grabbed the Weapon, and tossed it to Kai. "Now let's sneak out while those boneheads are still busy," he said.

Behind them, the statue's mouth slowly began to open. . . .

# AN ESCAPE GONE WRONG

The ninja walked outside of the cave . . . right into Samukai and his warriors!

Samukai opened all four of his arms wide. Each bony hand held a sharp dagger. The ninja drew their swords and charged ahead with a battle cry.

*"Hii yaa!"*

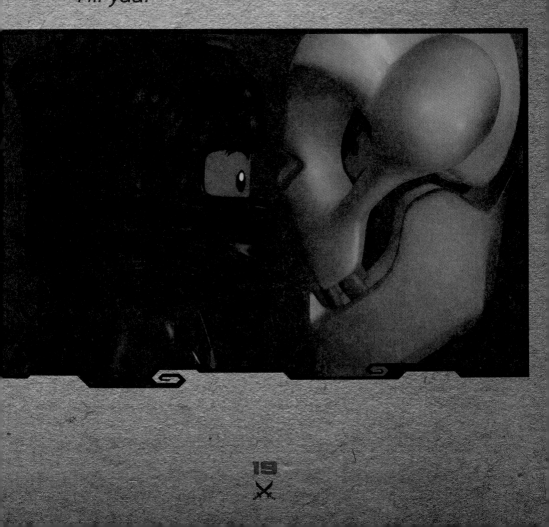

Cole, Jay, Kai, and Zane fought their way through the army of skeleton warriors.

"There's too many of them!" Kai yelled, whacking a skeleton with his sword.

"Let me handle it!" Jay called out. He jumped into the middle of a gang of warriors.

Suddenly, Jay stopped. He looked at the warriors in front of him. Some held long staffs. Others were spinning weapons above their heads.

"Guys, it's just like Sensei's training course!" he realized.

All four ninja had practiced on the course. They wanted to learn Spinjitzu. But so far, none of them could spin like Sensei Wu.

"Over the planks!" Jay cried, jumping from warrior to warrior, knocking them down.

"Dodge the swords!" Jay somersaulted over the heads of the sword-waving warriors.

"Here comes the dummy!" he finished, spinning into another warrior.

# MASTERS OF SPINJITZU

Jay kept spinning faster . . . and faster . . . and faster . . . until he became a glowing blue tornado.

"Spinjitzu!" Cole cried.

"Jay, what's the key?" Kai called out.

"I'm just going through the motions!" Jay yelled back.

Kai remembered the training. He jumped. He somersaulted. He spun . . . and he became a spinning tornado!

Cole and Zane got it, too. Soon all four ninja were using Spinjitzu, taking out skeletons left and right.

## ENTER THE DRAGON

"Retreat!" Samukai shouted.

The four ninja chased Samukai and his army out of the cave.

Cole flexed his muscles. "Guess they didn't want any more of these babies," he bragged.

Then they all heard a strange, growling noise behind them.

"Um, didn't Sensei say there was a guardian protecting the Weapon?" Zane asked.

The dragon statue wasn't a statue at all — it was a real dragon! The huge beast slowly rose to its feet.

"Is th-th-that what I think it is?" Cole asked nervously.

"I sense we will not be able to spin our way out of this," Zane remarked.

The dragon reared back, opened its mouth, and blasted the ninja with a blazing orange flame.

*"Aaaaaaaaaaaah!"* The ninja screamed as the blast knocked them down.

Cole, Jay, Kai, and Zane raced away as hot dragon fire licked at their heels.

Kai got a gleam in his eye. He removed the cloth that covered the Scythe of Quakes.

"Bad idea, Kai!" Jay warned. "Sensei told us not to use it."

　　But Kai didn't listen. He ran up to the dragon.

　　*Bam!* Kai swung the Scythe and brought it down on the cave floor. The ground began to tremble and crack. The dragon lost its balance and fell.

　　"We've got to escape!" Cole yelled.

# TEAMWORK

The four ninja raced away. But the dragon wasn't down for long. It started to chase them.

"We can use Spinjitzu!" Cole cried. He started to spin, and his friends did the same.

Soon four glowing tornadoes were swirling up the cave walls, heading for an opening in the ceiling.

Cole, Jay, Kai, and Zane escaped through the hole before the dragon could catch them.

"That was so awesome!" Cole cheered. He gave Kai a high-five.

"Yes! We are unbelievable!" Kai yelled.

"We are the best," Zane said proudly.

"Did you see that?" Jay asked. "I was like, *pow! Bam!*"

Sensei Wu joined the four ninja. "Kai, you are part of a team now. Do not forget that." Sensei turned around. "Come! There are three Weapons left."

The four ninja followed Sensei Wu out of the canyon. Now that they had mastered Spinjitzu, they were ready for their next adventure.